# NAKYTA'S GLITTER

## VOLUME III- WRATH OF NICOLE

## SIMPLY NICOLE

# DEDICATION

I would like to dedicate this book to everyone that said I would not amount to anything or become a successful business owner. To everyone that counted me out, judged and made me feel less than for being different. Hopefully, your souls find eternal peace. I implore everyone to recognize that words are spells and to use them to manifest greatness in yourself and others, not tear people down. The potter wants to use you again. There is an artist waiting to be discovered in all of us. Keep chiseling until that masterpiece is discovered.

~Ase~

# ACKNOWLEDGMENTS

First and foremost, I would like to give thanks to The Creator. I finally understand my purpose. Thank you for seeing me fit for this assignment.

In the words of Snoop Dogg,

"I want to thank me

I want to thank me for believing in me

I want to thank me for doing all this hard work.

I want to thank me for having no days off

I want to thank me for never quitting

I want to thank me for always being a giver and trying to give more than I receive.

I want to thank me for trying to do more right than wrong.

I want to thank me, for just being me at all times."

~Uncle Snoop~

I especially want to thank my loyal fan base that is incarcerated in DC, Maryland, Virginia, and Atlanta. I do it for you all. Gods got you. Believe that. I love you all.

# Introduction

## The Bear

Fuck me… Fuck me??? Nicole must have forgotten that I brought her in the world, and I can take her right on out. She may be an adult, but I am still her father and I command respect! I mean, I understand that she is mad at me because she thinks that I abandoned her. That is not the truth! The streets took me away from her. I am a man that lives by street codes. Some situations that I was in were unavoidable, or so I thought. Maybe it was my ego and arrogance that got me here. After all, no one should come before family and that is where I failed her. She is hurt and I caused a great deal of it. Unable to think straight or trust anyone, Nicole is in survival mode and prone to make careless mistakes.

She needs me more now than ever. I paced the floor of our cell at least 100 times pondering Montez's suggestion while he slept. He had suggested that I have a few inmates attack me bad enough so I would be sent to medical and once there I could come up with an excuse to be transferred to the local hospital. We would arrange a heist so that the transport vehicle carrying me would be intercepted. All that sounds good to me, and I am ready for a little danger, for ol' time's sake. There was only one problem that came to mind. Everyone in this facility respected me and would tear the head off the next man's shoulders if it looked like they were moving funny towards me. Who in their right mind would risk attacking me?

My mind wandered and before I knew it, I was teary eyed and thinking about the time I seen my baby girl graduate high school. I had done a short stint in prison but made it out two days before Nicole was set to graduate. No one knew I was released until it came time for her to walk across the stage. All I could see was that million-dollar smile that she flashed at me; when she looked up and seen me cheering from the stands as the announcer called her name as class valedictorian. Her speech received a standing ovation, and it was at that moment that I knew she would go on to do great things. She inherited her mother's smarts so anything she put her mind to she would achieve and master. Perhaps that is why I feel terror brewing in the pit of my core.

She is already a clever girl and now she is in survival mode. She will not know the strengths and lengths she can go to until her back is against the wall. The apple never falls far from the tree. NEVER! Both of her parents are bat shit crazy and at the end of the day, she is *Edwards* born. My mind is racing, and it does not help that Montez is asleep, as if nothing is going on. Time is of the essence, and he is getting his beauty rest. That's it, I need to call Nicole again! I must hear her voice and know that she is okay and does not hate me. I want to help her, but she needs to be willing to receive my help.

As gangster as I am behind bars and was in the streets, I am terrified. Never in my life have I ever frozen up or been scared. This shit hits differently. My daughter's life is on the line. There is no room for errors. For the first time in my life, I feel powerless. I need someone to tell me that it will be okay. Even if it is a lie, I need to hear it. Words of comfort in this trying time are paramount to my wellbeing. I keep replaying our conversation of me telling her to lay low. My nose started burning and before I knew it, I felt tears roll down my cheeks. It was a painful release that caused me to laugh, forcing salty tears into my mouth as I gasped for air. The realization of not shedding a tear since Nicole was born hit me like a ton of bricks.

It reminded me that I was still human and not completely heartless. Montez heard my wail and woke up. My heart was still racing at the thought of my baby girl being in imminent danger. After hearing the panic and hatred in Nicole's voice when she said, "Fuck you", I vowed that I would not waste another day behind the prison walls of *Noakwood*. Nicole was hurt and needed her dad. That is all a girl ever needs is her dad. Regardless of the tough act that she put on, I knew that she loved me and would listen to my instructions. Babygirl is just hot headed. She has been on her own for the most part. Montez and I talked for what seemed like hours. He expressed deep remorse for the role he played in Nicole's life.

As well connected as I am, I could not figure out who to call or what to do. Montez suggested that I get access to another phone and contact Devo over at *Orakee*. He also suggested that I go and talk to Warden Paul. Surely, he owed me a favor or two. I could sense Tez growing frustrated at me because I would not snap out of it. I spent my whole life being the fixer of other people's problems and here I sit, with cold feet. Tez yelled out,

"O.G., snap the fuck out of it bruh! Nicole is in trouble and needs our help. We need your head in the game O.G., where you at?" He was right, I needed to get my head in the game. It felt like the grim reaper was tugging at my heart. Nothing made sense to me anymore. My body and mind were in shock, and I did not even feel it when Montez punched me in the face. Before I knew it, I was getting up off the floor of my cell.

Still frozen in fear, I reminisced back to when Nicole was a little girl. I was leaving to go to the store, and she asked if she could go too. Instead of taking the car, we walked. Every bush or shrub we passed by; she was able to identify. As we approached the *Tic Toc* liquor store, I instructed Nicole to wait out front because the store was not appropriate for ladies. She agreed and as a reward, I took her to *Little Caesar's* and let her get whatever she wanted. On the way back home, she ate a package of cookies from the pizza shop and her mouth was dry afterwards. Stupid me passed her my *Budweiser* to drink, not realizing that I could be contributing to the start of an addiction. You think certain things are harmless in the moment. It isn't until later that you realize that your actions were wrong. What if I had bought her a juice and passed her that instead? There is no telling how that beer affected her adolescent brain.

There is so much that I wish I had taught her, so much that I wish I had said. If I never get the chance to say anything else to her, I just want her to know that I love her and am proud of her. Only if my actions lined up with my words. When she graduated high school, she went straight to nursing school. It is extremely hard to believe that her life has been reduced to what it has been. She was on the right track. My child was good, and Montez messed that up. What is more frustrating is that I cannot fault him. I was the same kind of man. That is how karma works. Sometimes karma will miss you and hit your children. That makes the suffering ten times worse. Everything that was sent to break her, she had to prevail through on her own, without my help.

Nicole is paying for my mistakes and in the process, I am suffering because I am in here as useless as a corn on a toe. FrootLoop came across my mind, and I thought about reaching out to her. That girl still worshipped the ground that I walked on. When she went to prison, it shook the core of our foundation; but I was determined to stay down and do right by her, because many times I had done wrong. She is eligible for parole in one year and I know she will get it this time. I came out of my thoughts and told Tez to get the warden for me. In the meantime, I stepped to a couple dudes that watched my back and explained that I would be leaving. If push came to shove, I would give my life so that my daughter could continue living hers, and I could accept that.

So many of my loved ones passed away since I've been locked up. I did not hear about the death until it was time for the funeral. Closure does not exist for people like me. Just like it did not exist for the loved ones whose family I took from them. Damn, I get it now. I took away the possibilities for so many people when I killed them. They never had a chance to right whatever wrongs they had made, they never had the chance to grow into what they were meant to be. The tears made their way from my eyes as Warden Paul walked into my cell. He looked genuinely concerned and walked me to his office where we could talk in private. There was not much that I needed to say to him. He is a family man and he seen the look in my eyes. A conversation took place between the two of us and no one opened their mouths.

I did ask to use a burner phone so that I could call FrootLoop, Nicole, LuAnn, and Devo. He gave me a phone and stepped out of the office. He may be the warden of the prison, but we have been friends since third grade. Some kids were bullying him at the playground, and I stood up for him. We have been tight ever since. The phone rang two times before Devo would answer. He let me know that people were talking about the murder of Judge Conyers and husband. They suspect Nicole could have done it but there is no actual proof. The security cameras had nothing on them. He said that a new judge had been assigned but could be paid off. If it was Nicole, then she would be on her way to the district attorney's house.

FrootLoop was not too thrilled to hear from me. She cussed me out and hollered about how she would fuck me up if something happened to her baby girl. That cheered me up enough to let out a laugh. All these years later and she is still the same. She did insist that I call her Latanya though. Something about wanting to be called the name she was given and not the name she earned. If that makes any kind of sense. Latanya or FrootLoop, the broad is still crazy. She told me that LuAnn had done some things that dishonored the family, and it surprised me because LuAnn had been the glue to the family since we both had been incarcerated. To hear that she had been sleeping with Montez disgusted me. There was no time to feed into the family drama, but I would not forget to address it.

It was all about Nicole and I would stop at nothing to see her to safety. When Nicole was 9, I took her on a vacation off the grid. It was a remote farm outside of Birmingham, Alabama. Growing up, Nicole expressed a love for elephants as young as one year old. I bought that farm because it had elephants. That was my gift to her and if she would just clear her head and think back, she would know what direction to go. I called Nicole and reminded her of that farm. She could seek refuge there and wait on me. Only the staff would be there, and they would never betray me. Not after all that I have done for them even with me being locked up. She would be relieved to know that she had somewhere to go and even more relieved that I had promised to meet her there.

# Chapter 1

## <u>Nicole</u>

Sit tight… Sit tight?? Life is not granting me the luxury of sitting tight. Who in the hell does my dad think he is? He may have run the prison and may have run the streets when he was out but this ain't that. It has been years since I have heard from him anyway. Why do men think that they could do that? Years have gone by without so much as an "I love you" from him. Exactly why I do not believe it when people say it to me. Suddenly, he thinks he can call and give me instructions like I am a toddler. Why hasn't he been calling me? Why now? I have been handling my shit on my own without his help for a decade now. He wants to be a parent to me now.

He has time to remember that I still exist. Well, that is cute! He is in there and I am out here, ALONE! Sit tight where? Until when? I love my father dearly. Once upon a time, he could tell me what to do and I would do it with no hesitation or question. One of the last good memories I have of my dad was the time he let me stay up late on a school night to watch *South Central* with him. That movie always brought us closer. We could talk about anything when we watched that movie. Imagine how I feel. One day I woke up and he was gone. Never to be heard from again until now.

He abandoned me for women, drugs, and the fast life. ME!!!! His baby girl. I often imagine how my life would have been if he had continued to put me first. What would I be had he stuck around to teach me how predatorial men could be when it was something they wanted? My dad could have put me up on good game because he was that nigga in the streets. Instead, he has me out here like a walking embarrassment. I got played yo!

I have very few memories of my maternal mother. She was arrested back in 1991. The way I feel, it was only a matter of time before that lifestyle caught up with me. There ain't no escaping certain shit that you were born into. My aunt did what she thought was her best with me, I think. There had always been a vibe of resentment between the two of us and I think this vibe came long before I did. I chose to ignore it because I did not think that blood could operate that way with each other. Boy was I a fool! The truth is that some people only do what is beneficial to them in that moment. The first question that pops into their head is, "What can I stand to gain"? That is a lousy way to think, be and live. I did not inherit that trait. It was not bad vibes one hundred percent of the time. LuAnn was a beautiful person, and she possessed a heart of gold; however, she could flip the switch in the blink of an eye.

She could go from hot to cold quicker than you could breathe in air. That was the ugly trait that I inherited from my mother's side of the family. I worked hard not to be that person. I will always be in debt to her for taking care of my children and I, in my time of need. Only God knows how much I miss Jenesis, Messiah and Angel. DAMN!!

My soul is weary and every day I stress about making my way back to them. Out of shock and disappointment, I took the kids away from LuAnn and sent them to stay with Tez's mother. The life that I was living had no room for raising children. I needed to be as heartless as possible to stay alive and after two days of having my babies, I made the difficult decision to send them away. They are a representation of true love in its purest form. They would more than likely end up as collateral damage and they deserved more from me than that. My life has fallen apart and my only two options are death or jail. As long as I had eyes that worked, I would kill you before you had the chance to kill me, so death really was not an option for me.

The anger and rage from the thought of my options, fueled the fire that led to me making the decision to kill Judge Conyers and whoever else stood in the way of my freedom. After taking my babies to Tez's mother, Ms. Lydia's house; Jenesis screamed and hollered as I tried to leave. Ms. Lydia said to me, "Leave and do not come back until everything is handled. Bring my son back home to me". In my mind, that was her way of giving me the green light to do anything, by any means necessary. Maybe I was wrong about her all this time. She seemed cool to me. I cannot help but wonder what Montez had been telling her.

If it is a front that she is putting on, her mask would eventually fall off. Angel began crying as Lydia handed me one thousand dollars and showed me the door. Mind boggled, I made my way down the driveway and to the local gas station to fill up and get two burner cells. I drove for about two hours and decided to get a room. I knew I could not check in under my name, so I pulled up on a girl standing near the hotel. As I rolled the passenger window down, I could not help but notice how beautiful this lady was. I asked her if I could pay her to get a room for a couple of nights and she agreed. Truth be told, I only needed one night to rest and plan my next move, it was her that looked in need of help.

While soaking in a hot tub, with *Childish Gambino's 42.26* playing on repeat, it became clear to me what I needed to do next. I called Rocco to catch up and ask a favor. I needed the address to Conyers house, and he delivered. We had agreed to meet up the next night and as always, he offered to help me. He said he would stake out the address to see what goes on and what time the judge went to work and came home.

After pouring a shot of *Courvoisier*, I anxiously went to sleep anticipating the next day to come. Rocco called me later the next day to say that he had been tailing the judge all day. She had left work and went to the bar with coworkers. He said that it would be a good idea for me to make my move to Conyers house and I did. Two hours had passed by and like clockwork, the judge had pulled into her driveway. There I sat, lurking in the bushes and before she could get out of her car, I walked up and shot into the window, killing her instantly. To my surprise, there was a man sitting next to her and he seen my face. I could not risk him identifying me in a line up, so I killed him too. My burner rang as I made my way back to my car.

After answering, Rocco gave me an address to meet up at. It would take four and a half hours to get back to New York from where I was, but I did not mind because he came through for me and did not have to. I went back to the hotel to shower and leave the key with the lady who had gotten me the room. I would later learn that her name was Dream, A dream she was too. Her skin was darker than milk chocolate, eyes were light as the sand on a beach, hair long and wavy, and she stood at five feet four inches tall. She seen me walk up to the room and followed me in. She shut the door behind herself and stood in my face eyeing me up and down before reaching in her pocket for a piece of tissue to wipe blood off the side of my face. As careful as I thought I had been, I was still clearly careless.

These are the type of mistakes that get people caught up. She stared into my eyes seductively and curiously at the same time. I broke the silence by asking her name and telling her mine. Dream asked me how I had gotten blood on my face and before getting up to take a shower, I said, *"Some things are better not knowing".* I handed her two hundred dollars and thanked her for getting the room. I expected her to be gone by the time I got out of the shower. Instead, she came into the bathroom, sat on the toilet, and lit a blunt. Dream asked that I tell her something about myself while passing the blunt. I drew a blank. She went on to tell me her story and how I came to meet her on the corner. Her girlfriend had put her out after suspecting that she had been using acid again.

She assured me that she was not using it and believed that her girlfriend just got tired of being with her.

That is how it goes. One day you wake up and you are just not in love anymore and you look for any excuse to break up with the other person instead of telling the truth.

**Lesson: No matter how far you may have come, some people will still choose to see you for what you used to be, and they will use it against you because they are not able to process your growth. Do not take it personally, keep on growing.**

Truth hurts though, so I probably would have done the same thing. There was an awkward silence as I thought about what I would tell her about myself. It was not anything interesting to say about myself except that I was who I was for a reason. *"I'm a survivalist Dream, my life was turned upside down a few months ago and now I do what is necessary to get by"*. Somehow, I felt like she knew what I was saying and before I knew it, she had pulled the shower curtain back, exposing her naked body. Her breasts sat up high and her nipples stood at attention. She stepped into the shower, softly brushing her body against mine. There was an instant connection between the two of us. As nervous as I was, I am still *Edwards* born. Once you step into my web, it is a wrap. You are mines until you are not.

My left hand lightly stroked her neck, and I used my right hand to pull her in close to me so that I could breathe into her ear. *"The bitches melt every time, trust me"*. She could tell that I had been through a lot and needed someone in my corner. A million thoughts ran through my head and the only thing I could say was that I had just killed the judge assigned to my case. Before I could get another word out, she kissed me on the mouth. As bad as I wanted affection, I did not kiss her back. Instead, I pushed her away and asked what she was up to. Dream got out of the shower without answering me and I was okay with that.

Hopefully, she would be gone when I got out of the shower. Maybe I hurt her feelings, women do not like being rejected. In all fairness, I did just meet her the day before. I was not looking for a fling. After putting on my sports bra and shorts, I exited the bathroom to see Dream and instantly thought, *"Damn, this broad is persistent"*. Maybe we both needed each other, and I just did not know it at the time. I certainly did not believe in coincidences, so I opened up to her a bit. Within one hour of me talking, she had dozed off. Tired was an understatement and I could not help but wonder what else she had been through. I went to my car to call Rocco and let him know what time to expect me. My intuition spoke to me, causing me to grab my little black bag from the trunk. Self said that it would come in handy.


As I made my way back into the room, I stumbled over a shoe on the floor, causing Dream to wake up. She apologized for falling asleep while I was talking and got up to pour me a drink. Little did she know that was a trigger for me. Dream turned on some music as I sat down on the bed and sipped my drink. She danced her way over to me while staring deeply into my eyes. *Sade's – Still in Love* played in the background. Damn, she knows how to grab a gal's attention. Her body spoke to me, it said that it needed to be touched and loved in a way that only I could do. I finished my drink and sat the glass on the floor. Her body moved effortlessly to the beat, and it turned me on.

She began removing her clothes, still gazing into my eyes and swaying her hips to the beat. I pulled her in towards me, and she straddled my lap. Dream gazed deep into my eyes and asked me to make her feel good. Like an excited dog, I stood up, with her still on my lap and laid her down. I climbed over top of her, passionately kissing her from her right collar bone to the center of her chest and then over to her nipples. My tongue moved in circles around her waistline, causing her body to rise and fall every time she felt my warm lips on her soft skin. It was at that moment that I realized that she needed me. By the looks of it, she was enjoying herself. I stopped kissing on her abdomen and made my way down to her inner thighs, causing her to let out a soft moan.

She grabbed me by my freshly cut head and directed me to her lotus flower. It was already soaking wet and that made me look up at her in awe. I kissed her pussy lips lightly and gently suckled on them. My tongue parted her two lips and circled around her clitoris in slow motions. Her nectar was to die for, and I feasted faster, careful not to cut her flower with my braces. As soon as I slid my thick warm tongue into the moist opening of her lotus flower, she squeezed my head, moaning loudly as she orgasmed in my mouth. Her fluids were clear, and the taste was exquisite. She most certainly had to be vegan, a raw vegan at that. I made a mental note to ask about her diet and pussy secrets later. In the meantime, I got up to get the bag I had retrieved from the car and went into the bathroom to assemble myself. I slipped into my black and purple *Nike* sports bra and my purple *RodeoH* harness briefs with the "O" ring.

After inserting my seven-and-a-half-inch realistic dildo, I returned to the bedroom. Dream bit her lip and motioned me to come over to her. With her legs still trembling from her orgasm, I turned her over on her side and slid inside of her as her body quivered. Dream had no idea what she was in for. My hips gyrated to the beat of every song that played for the next forty minutes, as she orgasmed time after time, every time I put her in a different position. She chanted self-affirmations in my ear as I got it in. Shit like, I am worthy of your love, I am Queen, I am God. When she dug her nails into my back, I flipped her over into doggy styled position. She bit into the pillows and gripped the sheets as I stroked her flower with all the love and hate I had in me. I was on the brink of experiencing an orgasm and knew that it would not be fulfilled completely unless I was looking into her eyes while she choked me.

In a hurry, I turned her over and put her hand around my neck as I pumped, prompting her to choke me. She got the message and choked me lightly and then harder, causing me to close my eyes and cum long and hard. When I closed my eyes, I saw the face of every life I took, and it turned me on. SINISTER! I fell asleep, still assembled and she did not mind. Dream wrapped herself in my arms and fell asleep too.

The next morning came, and I tried to wake up early enough to shower and leave without waking Dream. She had woken up before me and had been watching me sleep. As I opened my eyes, I saw Dream, staring at me and I smiled. In that moment, it felt good to be admired while sleeping. She sat on my lap and asked if I was leaving, and I said yes. Tears fell from her eyes as she began explaining that she was not in search of a one-night stand. She asked if I could take her with me. My life had no room for her or emotional attachments; but her pussy, her pussy was good as shit. I am talking about grade A good. I would have to make an exception. Her pussy gave me the motivation to make it back home another night just so I could taste it again and again. How could I say no to her? I told her that I had to go meet up with someone in New York and tie up some loose ends so that I would not spend the rest of my life in jail.

She still insisted that I take her with me. Dream went as far to tell me how well connected she was and how much I could benefit by having her around. She needed me and I needed her. We would have each other's back, and just like that, *"My watch begun"*. I engaged in a little more oral sex with her before driving to New York.

While driving, I asked about her lifestyle and vaginal health. She told me that she was vegan and twice a month, she visited *Ancestral Secret Essentials* in Washington D.C., for her yoni steam and care products. She explained that it was a black owned business; that focused on healing women naturally, without any pharmaceutical interventions.

**Readers: Close your eyes if you will. Imagine the scent of jasmine and chamomile. Now put a taste to**

**that, this time with a drop of honey and dash of fresh vanilla. Can you taste that? Now you taste Dream.**

My burner rang and to my surprise, it was my daddy again. He mentioned something about an elephant farm in Alabama that he had bought for me when I was a small girl. He promised to meet me there. Look at God. I did not care about how he would escape. All that mattered to me was that he was coming to save his baby girl. I may put up a hard act but deep down inside, I just want my daddy. I am his only child. I am sure that I am supposed to be a princess or something. This is his chance to fix that because this has been ghetto. Dream asked why I was so excited. I kissed her hand and asked if she liked elephants as I pressed my foot harder on the gas petal. I called Rocco to inform him that I would be taking a detour. He offered to help and the way I saw it, I needed allies. I told him where he could find me, and he promised me that he would be there within 48 hours.

# Chapter 2

## <u>Warden Paul</u>

The Bear and I go back like four flats on a Cadillac. When I was a small boy, children would pick on me because I wore glasses and had a squeaky voice. One day; while at recess, two sixth graders approached me and wanted to fight. O.G came from the other side of the field and beat the hell out of both boys. Ever since then, I never had a problem and the two of us became inseparable. We were lucky enough to be assigned to the same classes all the way until the end of high school. I joined the army after graduation and later went into corrections. He went on to take a different path. A part of me feels like I owe him my life. The kids in high school were extremely violent and relentless. For the past ten years, he's been at *Noakwood* facility under my care. The Bear rose to fame behind bars within two months of his being here.

If I had it my way, I would let him walk out of here today so that he could help Nicole. The man has more than paid his debt to society. Most of the time that he was sentenced to was because of his arrogance and ego, not the actual crime. He didn't know when to shut up.

During his trial, the judge was scolding him and O.G cut her off and said, "I put my pants on the same way you do". The judge asked, "and how is that"? O.G had the audacity to say, "Bitch, one leg at a mother fucking time"! She added an additional twelve years to the ten that he took a plea bargain for. Unfortunately, the judge wanted to make an example out of another black man, he made it easier.

The Bear is not the same man that he was ten years ago. He has humbled himself and even went as far as to mentor the younger generation of hotheads. Everyone has respect for him, even the staff. The Bear makes working here worth it, sometimes even fun. Somehow, he was able to get rival gang members to come to a truce. There is no violence or prison rape anymore; hasn't been a case of either in over seven years. Everyone here has a mutual respect for the fact that we were all men, fathers, sons, uncles and brothers. They just want to do their time and make it home safely to their loved ones. It made no sense to be fighting and killing each other. Now was a time as any to be empowering one another and lifting each other up, because serving time fucks with your head. Makes you depressed and what not. They aren't each other's enemies. They should be helping each other grow through that. The system is the real enemy and some of them play right into their hands, time after time.


When you look around, most of the inmates are black. Now don't get me wrong; there are Whites, Latinos, Asians, and even Pacific Islanders here. No one is exempt. What I am saying is that out of the mix, the majority are black. Why do you think that is? There's a plan put in place to eradicate the black population. They're locking up the brothers, hooking the sisters on drugs and turning the children gay. They're even turning brother against brother so that they kill each other. Sounds like an agenda to me! Slavery is still legal; and when you enter the penal system, you are their slave. Back in the day, it was the KKK that would kill little black boys and girls for sport. The men and women were not excluded. Today, the police do it for fun and sadly we do it to each other.

When Bear got here, the violence was unimaginable. He sat in the mess hall and watched a man drive a handmade shiv through another man's eye, for not giving up his dessert. He witnessed a black man kill a Korean guy because word on the tier was that he had raped his own mother. Everyone here has their own story. Some were brought up differently than others. There certainly are cultural differences that kept the facility divided for as long as I've been here. O.G was able to get everyone on the same page and way of thinking. Despite everyone's differences and what led them here; they were all men, that God chose to keep. Therefore, it was not up to the next man to decide who lives or dies. That was God's business. If you love your brothers as God loves you, you'd see that by killing your brother, you are part of the problem.

To keep O.G busy, I let him run a program, three times a week. Budgeting was tight and there weren't any programs put in place for rehabilitation or reform. Some of the men had a hard time with accountability. Half of the prison hid behind the Alford plea, and that is weak. It's this plea where you don't say you're not guilty, but you don't say that you're guilty. It's your way of not incriminating yourself and letting the courts prove what they can. Most people take this plea, understanding that there was enough evidence to take to trial. Some want to avoid that. What about the victims that were victimized? Sure, these men aren't the same as they were when they came in. Some struggled with drug addictions and did unthinkable things while under the influence. O. G's program helped these men get to the root of their problems and it almost always led back to a childhood trauma.

They were given the opportunity to confront their victims and offer sincere apologies. You'd be surprised how many rape victims and victims of domestic violence, sat blaming themselves for what their attacker did. That is a trauma that has the potential to change that person forever. Their attacker is in prison, and they are out with their physical freedom, yet they are mentally enslaved. Mental bondage is no different from physical bondage. I take that back. Mental bondage is far worse! O.G and I have one thing in common. We believe that everyone needs to get to a point in their lives where they can be accountable and give their victims closure.

Most of them are just waiting for that apology. They need to know that it wasn't their fault. They deserve that closure, and we have the power to give it to them. The ones that aren't deceased! It is also freeing to the inmates as well. They are weighed down with burdens and nightmares of the things they did to land them here.


There's no doubt in my mind that it is time to pay my debt to O.G. It's nearing the end of my shift and the start of my nine-week vacation. This would be the only chance that I would get to help him. I know he needs help, and his pride won't let him ask for it. I called on my most trusted C.O to bring O.G and Montez to my office. Within ten minutes time, the pair had arrived. Montez stood, clearly annoyed by O.G. This is the first time that I had ever seen him so disconnected from reality. Before I could say a word, Montez said, "Yo what the fuck man, are we just gonna stand here staring at this fool or are we gonna shake some shit'? I tossed O.G and Montez a pair of C.O uniforms from the closet in my office. That was the moment that O.G snapped out of it. I explained that my shift was over in twenty minutes.

There wasn't much that I could do to help them on the outside, but I could help them get out of here. All they had to do was go towards the laundry room and out the loading dock. There aren't as many cameras that way, and there was a van with keys on the dashboard waiting on them. I made sure they understood that once count came around, and they were found to be missing, that it would be a matter of time before their faces were plastered on every news channel. They would be considered fugitives at large and that type of charge would get you up to thirty years, once caught. My advice to them was to move fast and not get caught. Once Nicole was safe, the only option they had was to get passports and get the hell off American soil. It's time to move!

We said our goodbyes and they left my office under the guise of correctional officers. I stayed behind to wipe the camera footage that showed them being escorted to my office. All the correctional officers loved O.G, so I am confident that they will wait until the last minute to do the count. They have a good head start. The rest is up to them. I am off to Bermuda. My vacation is for nine weeks; however, I know I will not be returning. Secrets are going to be revealed. When O.G and Nicole encounter one another, she won't help but remember things about her father that everyone thinks she forgot. She's shared quite a bit of those secrets with me. We've all got our secrets. There are things that I did and was done to me that I want to carry to the grave. The Bear is no different.

He can't take back what he did; but he's not going to let what he did define who he is becoming. I would never hold a man's past against him. Some could say that I am a part of the problem. I'd much rather believe that I am a part of the solution. I've dedicated my life to prison reform. God granted me a second chance and so far, I have made good on my promise to myself. I am pleased with my actions and can only hope that come judgement day, my creator will be pleased and commend me for a job well done. If there was ever any mistake that I wanted to correct; it would be how I chose to raise my daughter Lyric. I was not there for her, and I regret it. God willing, I will be given a second chance to make things right between the two of us. I have made a positive impact on countless people that come through these doors. My only wish is that they pay it forward. Be the change that they wish to see. I'm tired of seeing my people fail.

# Chapter 3

## <u>Rocco</u>

The first time that I met Nicole was a little bit informal. The homies and I were standing outside of the Gardens when I seen a cutie from the back. Like any man, I tried to shoot my shot, not realizing who she really was. She took offense to my approach and pulled a gun on me. She had a .57 on my nose. A little feisty mama. My heart skipped a beat. She would need assistance getting rid of a body and later taking a life for her protection. I believe that she thinks that I am just an ordinary guy that works for Ken, cleaning up situations. After seeing and hearing her talk, I realized that that was The Bear's daughter, Nicole.

I took my orders from him, and the order was to protect his baby girl even if it cost me my life. I owed that man my life and was willing to lay it down for his daughter. It's her feistiness that draws me in. How unfortunate that that's The Bear's daughter. As bad as I wanted to push up on her I didn't. I would be violating. I did three years with O.G at *Noakwood*. He's saved my ass more times than I can remember. He is the reason that my time was reduced, and he helped me come to terms with what I had done.

Doing the crime is one thing; being able to accept the role you played and apologize for your actions, well that's another thing. Just like most of the men at *Noakwood*, I didn't have my father or mother to raise me. I jumped off the porch at seventeen and began selling drugs. I didn't care who I was selling it to if it made me money. Huge mistake! A cat had overdosed on a bad batch of molly that I had sold him and nearly died. Had I been eighteen, they would have thrown the book at me. Under the juvenile guidelines, the maximum sentence they could give me was seven years. Good behavior would shave off some of that time. I did one year in juvie before I was transferred to *Noakwood* and met O.G.

At first, my attitude was that it wasn't my fault that motherfuckers wanted to get high. Time with O.G had changed my perspective. I was killing my own people by supplying that shit. Drugs ain't never been my thing, neither has alcohol. I don't understand how people could get hooked on that shit. You gotta have hella demons haunting you to get addicted to anything. O.G caught me in time and taught me how to clean my closet and release the burdens that kept me bound. As a result, I was a free man three years before my time. He asked me for two favors; pay it forward and answer the phone when he calls. He didn't have to call about Nicole, I recognized her peanut head ass because she was a splitting image of her dad. The low hair cut highlighted their resemblance. Nicole doesn't know it yet, but as soon as she touches down, I have a surprise for her.

Detective Aldez and Boone are chained up in the warehouse at the back of the Gardens. These are the detectives that Montez cut a deal with. My homie has ears in high places and with a little monetary persuasion, she gave me the names and addresses of everyone assigned to Nicole's case. It's gonna be a reunion to die for once she arrives. In the meantime, I'll continue staking out a few addresses that I got leads on.

Within one hour of my stakeout, Nicole called to say that she was one hour away. Shortly after that, my burner rang again and to my fucking surprise, it was O.G.

He was out and in search of Nicole. Everybody has got their triggers and in all the time that I've known O.G, this is the second time that I heard this tone from him. The first time that I heard genuine remorse and regret in his voice was after he opened up to me about his daughter and the things he did. I'll never utter those words out of my mouth. Hearing his tone, then and now, makes me want to protect Nicole as I would my sister, mother, daughter or lover. How can a man call himself a man and not want to protect the black woman. They're becoming extinct too! That's another story line that most of us aren't ready to focus on. We'd rather be blinded by the glitz and glamour that celebrities portray on social media.

Meanwhile, back at the warehouse, I began to tidy up a bit as I waited for Nicole to arrive. Thoughts of how we first met kept replaying in my head.

Nicole wasn't from New York but on that day, you couldn't tell. Something about the way she had said, *"Disrespect me like that again and its lights out for you B, dead ass son"*, left me intrigued by her. Anticipating her arrival, I phoned Ken to let him know that it was time. Still mesmerizing over Nicole, I wondered if she would have a Déjà vu moment once she realizes that the warehouse is at the back of *River Gardens*. I unchained and unlocked the room that Aldez was in. He let out a loud shriek when he seen me standing at the door. After removing the gag from his mouth, he asked where he was and what the hell was going on. This man even had the audacity to say what he would do to me once he was untied. Why he thought he would live past tonight was beyond me. I was courteous enough to let him use the bathroom.

Regardless of the line of work you're in, you still gotta have dignity. Aldez didn't respect that dignity that I shared with him. He talked shit the whole time and it got under my skin enough for me to pistol whip him into silence. *"Next time you can piss and shit yourself"*, I yelled. While walking Aldez back to the chair I had him tied to, I decided to put a little pressure on him for the inconvenience. Word has it that he had twisted some of the words of character witnesses to make it seem like Nicole's family was turning on her. No doubt, both Montez and Lu said a little too much according to Nicole. I understand the reasons why the both of them broke. In LuAnn's case, she only talked once they shut down her business and threatened to take Nicole's kids from her. I can't speak on Montez too much, but I will say this, that rape shit… Mann ain't no fucking way in the world.

Anyhow, I told Aldez that I had a parting gift for him that was to die for. He had no idea that I had Boone in the room next to him. I didn't bother gagging him this time because I wanted to hear everything he would have to say. "This is gonna be so good", I said as I turned to walk away. Before I could get to the door, he let me know that I was a dead man. He went on to say how his partner would find him and kill me. He must have thought that I was a rookie. *"Now when you say your partner; do you mean your work partner, your lover, or both"*, I asked. His eyes grew extremely large, and I could see the terror and fear in them. I did my research well enough to know that his "partner" was really his lover. So much for the fraternization policy with employers and employees within a company. You wouldn't believe the shit that people talk about when they are afraid. They come across so boldly, like God herself can't stop them.

Well, Aldez is about to meet his maker; but before that, I'll taunt and torture him. Just until Nicole gets here. *"Give me a second gangsta"*, I said to Aldez before exiting the room.

He damned near had a heart attack when I came back into the room with a hooded lady chained by the hands and neck. Who could it be? "Aldez, remember you said what all you would do to me and the family that you think I have"? I asked. As soon as I revealed the hooded lady he begged and pleaded for mercy. He apologized for making empty threats towards me almost immediately. *"Kill me, just leave her out of it"*, he pleaded. The look I gave him let him know that his suggestion was not possible.

*"Aldez my man, I bet you didn't see this coming now did you? I can guarantee that you won't see what's about to come next. Me and Boone got real acquainted in the next room. She's quite a freak and I can see why you two are entangled"*. Secrets are about to be revealed to

them both and by the time this is over with, I am sure that the pair will feel like they've been sleeping with the enemy. *"Here's what I'm gonna do for you Aldez; I'm gonna let you watch as I fuck this bitch and make her eat my dick. You can scream all you want, no one will hear you"*. I turned to Boone and instructed her to get on her knees. She happily obliged. With her hands still in chains, she looked over at Aldez and swallowed my dick whole.

His mouth dropped in disbelief. I'm willing to bet that she didn't do this to him. My God her lips feels like pillows. I moaned as I grew rock hard in her mouth. I asked Aldez if it felt this good when she did him. The more she moaned, the harder I grew, and I was about ready to fire away but told her to stop and get on her knees while facing her lover. The moment I penetrated her, she let out a soft moan that told me she enjoyed it. I was dogging the pussy and talking shit the whole time. *"I can tell you wasn't hitting this thing right. Look at how she's enjoying me. I bet she don't look at you the way she is now"*.

He tried his best not to look but it was the only place that he could look. Seconds later she came all over my dick and I could feel myself cumming, so I pulled out, stood up and walked over to Aldez and shot my load on the bridge of his nose and mouth. Talk about disrespectful! I chained Boone up to the chair next to Aldez. The two of them would have some choice words for each other.


Normally when my phone rings, I retreat to privacy. Not this time, my adrenaline is pumping so I answered in front of the two of them. It's O.G! This time he was looking for his brother, Ken, my birth father. I didn't meet him until shortly before I turned eighteen. Before I knew he was my father, I began selling drugs for him. After my sentencing, he felt the need to unburden himself by telling me the truth. He also told me that O.G was his older brother. You guessed it, "The Bear" is my uncle, making Nicole my cousin. I always wondered why my father was never in the picture but understood at the same time. He chose the streets over family to keep us safe. Unfortunately, that's the same road Nicole is on, and I just want to help her get back to her family as soon as possible.

My father and I never had that uncomfortable conversation about his absence. It has been five years since we have known each other and we have a strict business relationship, so I conduct myself accordingly. I don't call that nigga my father or address him as dad or pops. Just Ken! Cold world ain't it?

The two detectives began to argue once I got off the phone. I could hear Aldez say something to the tune of it looked like Boone enjoyed fucking a random stranger. I glanced over at her and waited to hear her response. Turns out that she loved every bit of it and wanted more. When asked what she liked the most, she said, *"sucking his dick, it was so thick and long"*. I could not contain my laughter. That's a female for you. They will kick you when you are down. Why is she taunting this man? She yelled out for me to let her know when it was time for round two. This bitch is bold and crazy and that's just how I like them. The pair argued back and forth, and it drove me insane. This was worse than a fucking soap opera.

Where in the fuck are Ken, O.G, and Nicole's asses at? I'm about to lose my mind. Boone asked what was the reason that we were being held and Aldez told her that Nicole was more connected than they had suspected.

Boone had her eyes on one target ever since the murder of her baby brother. You guessed it; Albert "Al" Gibbs, and everyone knew that Nicole killed him. She doesn't know that Nicole will be arriving shortly. I am willing to bet that there will be a cat fight. While Boone and Aldez went back and forth over who did what to whom; Ken called to let me know that he had talked to "The Bear", and that he should be arriving momentarily. Ken had to make sure shit was quiet out front before he made his debut. Now it's time to get the party started. Seconds later, I heard a horn blow and that prompted me to raise the garage door. O.G and someone sitting next to him pulled up in the dopest, custom painted burgundy BMW 745i with chrome twenty-two-inch rims. I don't know how he has the pull that he does, especially considering that he was just incarcerated two days ago.

The shit was mad fly, and I could tell it had just been detailed. He pulled into the garage and my mouth watered at the mere sound of the engine. Bear parked the car, and he must have hit a hydraulic switch because the car went up and then glided down off some pimp shit. Both driver and passenger side doors opened.

O.G hopped out of the car first, grinning ear to ear. He hasn't aged that much; either he got shorter, or he wasn't as big as I thought he was, but I am sure the last time I saw him he had both front teeth. I noticed that one was missing. I offered to take him to a good periodontist that I had visited once or twice in the past. We dapped hands and hugged each other before he would say, *"oh Roc let me introduce you to Tez. That's my daughter's boyfriend or however it goes. My grandkid's father"*. I know bits and pieces from Nicole, enough to not do any kind of business with him. As I'm told, he's the reason for all this mess as it is. Montez got out of the car on Bear's command and introduced himself while holding his hand out as if he was waiting for brotherly love or some shit from me.

There I stood, with my arms folded and a mean mug on my face; not interested in a pow wow. This is one goofy looking dude. I am not sure what Nicole was thinking in the first place. We going to war over a nigga that betrayed his friend by hooking up with his girl when he went to prison. Then he cheats… WAIT! Nicole did say that she had recently found out that her marriage to this nigga was bogus. He was already married. So, a married nigga hooks up with my cousin; gets her pregnant while living two lifestyles, gets locked up and fucked by the man he betrayed, cuts a deal with the detectives that I have in the other room, seduces Nicole's aunt and drain her of her finances, goes back to prison and teams up with O.G on a mission to save Nicole.

This shit is so messy that even I can't keep up. All these motherfuckers are stupid if they can't see that he needs to be killed first. Self, self, self is all I see when I look at his bitch ass. He is only for self. He will do whatever for self, he will cross whomever for self. I'm not dapping this snake up.

The Bear broke my train of thought by saying, *"C'mon nephew, we all here for the same reason. Let's put our differences aside and find some common ground"*. "NIGGA WHAT! Fuck that philosophical, mentor the youth shit that you're tryna be on. This ain't *Noakwood*. This is the streets homie. That shit may have worked for the niggas you were locked up with but this ain't that. This the real-world blood! Too many passes have been given to this nigga on the strength of who he knows. He's a fucking snake and the more chances he gets to shed his skin, the larger the snake in him gets. Eventually he will devour us. Why can't anyone see that? C'mon man unc, prison done made you soft. Let me kill this fool now. This one is on the house", I yelled. Before anyone could say anything, a horn blew. That had to be Ken or Nicole. I am not a betting man, but my money was on Nicole.

She has been on the way since forever. *"Unc, I am disgusted that this nigga is still standing, and you are taking up for him"*, I said before turning around to open the garage door.

Good thing that I am not a betting man because it was my father, also known as Ken. As soon as he got out of the car, I started to vent. "Man, Ken man, prison done made uncle Bear soft", I said. Ken's eyes grew big and before I could say another word, he had punched me in the mouth and yelled how I was never to disrespect his brother. He's ranting about his brother like he's some kind of fucking legend. The way I'm feeling, I wouldn't mind making that nigga history for siding with the enemy. I know all about him and he's another snake for real for real! I understand that he may have turned over a new leaf. Shiddd back in his day he was all about self too. Anything he could do to benefit himself, he did it. On top of that, he was the type that did not ask, he just took. Perhaps that's why him and Montez clicked so well. Two fucking snakes, what are the odds?

*"Oh, so that's how it is around here pops? A man can't express his opinion"*, I asked. Bitch ass nigga ignored what I had said and went over to embrace his brother. It must've been twenty plus years since they last roamed the streets together. I can only imagine that they have a lot of catching up to do. I stepped off to give Nicole a ring. It has

been over an hour, and she should've been here by now. *"Whad up gangsta, where you at"*? She said she was about five minutes away. I told her to make it two minutes because she wouldn't believe who was here. She asked me to tell her but all I could say was that she would have to see for herself. I heard a voice in the background and asked who that was. She laughed and told me to mind my business. *"Imma just stay on the phone until you get here"*, I said. Nicole said, "Oh, whatever is going on must got you tight dada". *"Yeah man, you got surprises behind two doors. At this point, it's Christmas in June Nicole"*. "Fool, it's April", Nicole blurted out.

We both laughed until our faces hurt. She said, "Let me in". I did, and when she got out of the car, I said, *"You know, I gotta keep you on your toes baby girl, make sure your mind stays sharp"*.

# Chapter 4

## <u>The Reunion</u>

After greeting Rocco, I walked back over to the car and asked Dream what she wanted to do. She had the option to take the car and what little money I gave her to start over. She was also free to stay here with me and see how it all played out. I don't expect to be free much longer and I am not willing to take an innocent person down with me. Funny that I even trust her enough to walk away knowing that she knows a lot at this point. I've done enough damage as it is. It's to the point where my only options are death or jail. If you haven't figured it out by now, I am not going out without a fight. Dream gave me a disappointing look that I understood all too well. What she does not fully understand is that I will forever be a liability. My life is a complete disaster. Every excuse I gave her for us to part ways, she gave solutions and reasons as to why she would stay with me. She gave me hope and all I could feed her was partial truths.

I didn't tell her any blatant lies however I did not reveal all the truth. She was on a need-to-know basis! Some shit just ain't everybody's business and I am sure she has some shit that I don't know about. How couldn't she, we had just met! One thing that was for sure, she was staying, and I could not talk her into leaving. I took Dream by the hand, and we walked over to Rocco, and I introduced her to him as my girl. Stupid him asked Dream where his girl was at. The three of us stood there laughing until I noticed Rocco's face turn seriously cold. It was literally half a second after he finished laughing before his face told me that there really wasn't anything funny.

*"What I gotta pull my gun on you again Roc? Fill me in, don't keep me in suspense fool"*. He looked at Dream and then at me before saying, "alright hear me out; this the thing, my father and your father are brothers, born from the same mother". I could feel myself get annoyed and I said, *"OK, SO... I know you ain't call me all the way here to tell me that we're cousins. That's it, that's the big reveal"?*

"Nawl man, shut up and listen, Rocco yelled. They are in the other room and that's not all. Your father brought that goofy nigga Montez with him. I'm telling you cuz on the code, imma kill that nigga. That's just half the story; remember I told you I had something for you? I got them two dirty detectives in the room back there. What you wanna do with them? I say we pop that bitch ass nigga first. Oh, and one more thing man something is up with your pops man. He seemed too friendly with that clown and had the nerve to come at me off some philosophical mentoring shit, trying and get me to speak to his bitch ass. Now I understand that is your kids' father, but on the code he gotta go slim. I'm telling you because your father is weak".

Wait wait wait, this is way too much to process. My head is spinning out of control, and I can feel the blood boiling in my veins. Did he just say that Montez is in the other room? My father is here? My father is here! For some reason; as weird as it sounds, that is the only news that matters to me. Regardless of his past, he is here for his baby girl. Dream axed me if I was OK and what I wanted to do. I looked at Rocco and told him to lead the way. As we walked down the hall, Roc turned towards me and suggested that I deal with family matters first and I agreed. "Let the cards fall where they may baby", I said to Dream as Rocco opened the door that led to people that I love and hate.

The chatter stopped instantly, and everyone stared at me as if they had seen a ghoul. My birth father yelled out "what's up baby girl", as he walked over to me grinning and reaching out for a hug. My mind could not believe what my eyes were seeing. I declined the invitation for a hug and broke my silence by saying; "Last I checked, you still had a few more years on your sentence. How are you here in front of me? Why are you here in front of me? Why are you with an enemy of mine? Both of y'all were locked up together, right? Well, how was he still alive"? The more questions that I asked, the more I had, and I didn't even give him time to answer any of them before moving on to the next.

"Baby girl, I am here because you are my child and I love you. No jail sale in the world could keep me. You were in trouble, and I did all that I thought to do in order to be here for you. Any man put in the same position would do the exact same thing for their child. I am offended that you would ask. Furthermore, who is this girl that you're holding hands with? You two seem strangely close". Just because I knew that he did not condone lesbian and gay anything, I did not hesitate to introduce Dream as my lady. That smile he was wearing turned upside down instantly that low key brought me a great deal of satisfaction. Knowing that he could not do anything about my preference in partners was satisfying enough. To see his facial expression was near priceless to me.

"What do you mean she is your woman? I am not sure if you are aware that you yourself are a woman and furthermore you are an *Edwards*". We don't get down like that! Instant rage filled my body. Who was he to tell me anything about the cursed *Edwards* name like it's a badge of honor or I should be proud of? Nothing but shame and disgrace comes from my lineage. Fuck that name and fuck him. I'm not one to disrespect my elders, but truth be told he does not deserve my respect. If we must resort to the back and forth then so be it. What he won't do is stand here and scold me like I am a child because he doesn't agree with my sexual preference. Need I remind him that I took the straight route before. Look where it got me! It's been calamity after calamity ever since I had my first child. Who wants to keep living like that?

Women are cheaters, absolutely! Typically, they won't or don't cheat until the emotional connection is gone. Whereas with men, a ball mouth bitch with a phat ass and an eye in the middle of her forehead will make them risk it all. Just because it's something different, something new to them. I have heard plenty of people say that men are conquerors. In my opinion, getting pussy is not an achievement, what in the fuck did they conquer or achieve? Who in the hell came up with that bullshit?

"What do they call you? The Bear, O.G, I asked. Let me break it down for you really quickly so we can get down to real business. Your opinion of who I choose the date does not matter to me nigga. With all the years that have passed us by, you would think that you would be more accepting of me. I am your daughter and I love you without a doubt but don't get me wrong daddy, I am not pressed to have you in my life. Your secrets will always remain safe with me. Do not think for one minute that you do not play a role in my sexuality. Fathers are supposed to protect their children, not…".

"Baby Girl, this isn't the time or place for that. This is the time to handle business and make it so that you can have a fresh start", O.G yelled! He knew I was two seconds away from revealing the truth of why he was incarcerated. "Yeah, Ok nigga", I said while cutting my eyes at him and turning to Rocco.

Rocco gave me a confused look. You could tell that he knew something was up between Bear and me. I have never been one to cry over spilt milk, so a lot of things I let ride because I'm not a confrontational person. I just rather keep the peace, even if it means not bringing up the things that E me alive inside. There's a commandment that says that we are supposed to honor our mothers and fathers so that our days may be longer. I hate my father for what he's done, but I love him because that's what I want to do. When I was a little girl, he would let me hang out with him past bedtime and we would watch our favorite movie together. *South Central!* Come to think about it; that's where he got his name from. There is a character by the name of *"OG Bobby Johnson"*, that was about the street life and was rider die for his friends. He did his time and related turn his life around for the sake of his son. There was another character that went by the name of Bear.

He was the henchman in the gang. My father has clearly embodied the role of these characters from my favorite movie. Bear was his favorite actor in the movie and when he found out that he died in real life, he took on that name.

A huge part of me is waiting for my life to end the way the movie did. There is built up resentment between him and I. Mainly because he has turned over a new leaf and devoted his life to mentoring his jail friends but left me hanging. I do not mean it sounds selfish but what about me? His only child! When will he pour into me? People don't understand that their lives will never go right when they do not do right by their children. He has made me feel like I am disposable, and This is why we are here today.

I asked Rocco to show me what was in the other room. Bear and Dream had a worried look on their faces as we walked down the hall. We all approached a door at the end of the hall and Rocco yelled out for me to brace myself before opening the door. A part of my soul burned when he opened the door and I saw the face of someone I once knew. Sweat ran profusely down my forehead and neck. O.G asked what was up with me and robbed had went to get me a bottle of water. "This is too much for me. So much has happened in one day. I need a moment to process all this shit", I said. This is the first time that I have ever had an experience seeing a ghost. I have heard of instances where people would say that they see the ghost of the first or second person they had killed. What if this is what I am experiencing? For some people, there ain't no coming back from that.

Meanwhile, Boone is grunting loudly through the gag over her mouth. I can see that Rocco had beaten the hell out of Aldez. That made me laugh. He must have been talking shit and it got under Rocco's skin. Ever since my encounter with Aldez, I knew he was arrogant. You would think that he had simmered down while being held captive. Boone is still grunting which causes Rocco to get annoyed and he asked, "Yo Cole, what do you want me to do with this bitch". "I need her alive just until I can figure out who she was", I said. "Alright let me end the suspense and tell you that she is the sister of Albert Gibbs, aka, Al", he yelled. I walked in her direction while staring at her. They definitely resemble each other, perhaps that's why she kept grunting through the gate. I wonder what she has to say. Rocko warned me not to remove the gag, but I needed to know what she wanted to say to me.


There I stood; eye to eye with the female version of Al. Were they twins? I wondered while staring at her. Lost for words; I removed the gag from her mouth and before she could speak, she spat in my face and yelled MURDERER! Visibly upset, Dream hit her with the butt of her gun, which I never knew she had. It didn't stop Boone from saying what was on her mind. She has some choice words for me about the events that led up to her brothers' death. Of course, she blamed me. Afterall, I am the one who killed him. The more she talked, the better I felt for killing him. He was a liability and had to be dealt with accordingly. There ain't that much love in my heart for anyone that crosses me or tries to hang me out to dry.

It turns out that Boone's partner, Aldez had brought Al for simple questioning. You know, routine shit following the death of Nakyta. They questioned any and everyone connected to me after viewing my phone logs and illegally tailing me. If you remember, I had reached out to Al via phone, just to let him know that I was on the way to him. Our call was under 30 seconds.

That's how I knew that I was being followed. Moments later, I realized that I still had my phone on me and warned Al. He shut everything down and we both fled. My location was made and that was the start of Al's disloyalty. I reckon that Aldez and Boone played good cop, bad cop with him. Boone being the good cop. There ain't no sense in me trying to piece this shit together now. It's a done deal! The way I see it, I may as well taunt her over the death of her brother. Give her the grim details, just to get her a riled up before killing her. Something about hearing a pig squeal satisfies my soul. No one knew that about me! Not Jesse, Rocco, Dream, Montez or O.G. Only Al. This one is for you big homie!

# Chapter 5

## "Can't live without my heart"

With all the confusion and mayhem going on now; Dream noticed that I had broke out in a cold sweat and asked that we leave. Normally, I would finish business before departing but this time was different. Seeing my father standing in front of me is really taking me back. The memories keep flooding my mind and I cannot shut them off. It's like removing a band aid from a wound that you knew would never heal. Anyone that really knows me knows that I can be relentless and cold hearted if put in a tight spot. This is that! All I have done so far is stand in disbelief. I keep seeing glimpses of my childhood and my father has the lead role. Funny thing is, that man hasn't been in my life since I was eighteen. Years have passed and somehow, I am still eighteen, just waiting for my daddy to come to my rescue.

I turned to Rocco and asked him to hold it down in my absence. I needed to get as far away from everyone as possible. Just for one night! My mind and body required solitude. He agreed to hold it down; and on the way out, O.G9, as they call him, asked what was going on and where I was going. With my mind still in disarray, I turned to him and asked if he meant what he said when he told me that he couldn't live without his heart. His facial expression said it all. He wasn't expecting me to remember certain things that he had said and done. An elephant never forgets.

Years ago, when I was a small girl, my father would read to me before tucking me in to bed. As a child, I did not know that over half the books that he held in front of him at story time were not being read. Instead, he made up his own stories and at the end of each book, he would always tie that phrase in. As an adult, I would read some of the same books to Jenesis; and wondered what my dad had read to me because his version and the version I had read, never aligned. He made up stories to keep me engaged. Now that I think about it, he was telling me stories about his life. Those stories also included my birth mother. He called it, "Who took my FrootLoops". It was his way of telling me that my mom didn't leave, she was taken for circumstances out of her control. How clever! It went right over my head until now! Suddenly, I feel nothing but remorse for the way that I treated her. I shut her out of my life before I graduated high school.

One day, a kid in high school had seen me visiting my mom in prison and thought it be funny to embarrass me in front of the class. While on a visit with her father and I with my mother; we passed each other in the hallway. She didn't say anything to me there; but when we got to school and she got around her friends, she embarrassed me and hurt my feelings to the core. We were in the cafeteria when she said, "It's a good thing that you got your looks from your daddy, cuz I seen your mama and prison has made her ugly". Barely able to process her mean words, so I engaged in my first school fight. The crowd was cheering her on as she grabbed me by the hair and tried to overpower me. I wouldn't let up.

I reached for my tray of food and slapped her with it. She fell in a seated position, and I took that tray and kneed it into her face about four times. I utilized those boxing skills that my dad forced on me and beat the shit out of her.

Due to the manner of the fight and her injuries, I was expelled. The school board was not concerned that I had a stellar record or that she had started the fight, only that I had finished it. Now that I think about it, I am blessed that expulsion was all that I got. She had missing teeth, a broken nose, and fractured ribs from me picking her up from the floor and flinging her into the radiator that stuck out of the wall. The good news is that she did not bother anyone else. No one was afraid of her anymore. That was the power that made her tick. Instilling fear into people and scaring them into submission. Not me though, the bitch bleeds just like everyone else.

That was a lesson for all who witnessed. Do not fuck with the quiet ones, because when we react, you are going to wish that you had left us alone. I went to another school. That fight went on my record, but it did not stop me from graduating with honors and as class valedictorian.

LuAnn helped my father to raise me. He was in and out, mostly out, and I wondered if that had caused the resentment between Lu and I. Anytime my dad would show up, he would come through the door yelling, "What's up baby girl", as he picked me up and threw me into the air before catching me. Then he would hug me and say that soon I would outgrow him. LuAnn would always side eye us. It was as if she knew something about my dad that I did not. It had gotten so obvious to me one day and my dad asked me what was wrong after seeing my facial expression change. I told him that aunty always looked upset whenever he would come to see me. He did not dismiss my concerns and went to talk to Lu. Next thing I knew, he was packing my clothes and rushing me out of the house and into the back seat of his car. I must have been around eight.

Since it was close to summer break, my dad decided to take me to Langley Park Md, to spend time with the lady he was dating. This was just another way to get someone to take care of me while he ran the streets. Amber was her name, and she was not stupid. Although she was very kind to me, she knew what my dad was up to. Over the next few days, they would get into arguments because he was always gone. Other than doing hair, Amber had no idea how to take care of children. She didn't have any of her own, so I suppose that she did her best. Amber was kind to me. We painted each other's nails and took walks to the park or pizza shop. One night, maybe two weeks into my visit; my dad had come in while Amber and I slept. I heard the bedroom door close and then I heard banging and moaning sounds. Scared by the commotion, I went to sit in the hallway of the apartment building. My assumption was that when they were done, my dad or Amber would come looking for me.

About an hour later, my dad came to get me, and we sat in the living room watching *South Central*. He put me on his knee and apologized for being gone the whole day. Then he handed me the can of *Budweiser* that he was drinking. You could tell that he wished that I were a boy. He laughed at the character named *Loco* in the movie. No words were exchanged but I understood the vibes, even as a child. He passed me his can of beer and to this day, I wish that he hadn't. That's what connected us in his absence and it's what kept me bound and in this cyclic phase. I've been stuck at age eight since I was eight and never knew it until now. After *South Central* went off, he seen that I was still very much awake and put on *Blow* with *Johnny Depp*. Even as a child that movie impacted me for a lifetime.

The little girl fighting for her father's time and attention was me. Amber did not like the fact that my dad was bonding with me, so she started an argument that would turn physical, and she ended up putting the both of us out at around 3:00 AM with no regard as to where we would go.

My dad wasn't going out without a fight though. He delayed the argument until about 4:30 AM. I remember sitting in the living room *crying* as I continued to watch *Blow*. *Johnny Depp* had just been set up by his friend and on *his* way from the bathroom he was arrested. He never got the chance to pick his daughter up from *school*. During a visit to see her father in prison, the girl said to him; "I thought you said that you couldn't live without your heart" and walked off. That scene stuck with me for several reasons. Whenever me and my dad would part ways, he would always say that phrase to me. On that night at

Ambers, that was the last thing he said to me before the police hauled him away.

Turns out, he had broken some of Amber's ribs and blacked her eye for talking bad about me. She wanted him to herself and did not like the fact that I was there. My adolescent mind could not process that he was wrong for putting his hands on a woman even though he was sticking up for me. Now my adult mind understands it further, and yet, I still side with my father.

She was wrong for treating me like she did so fuck her. I'm not sure if that's all a part of me just sticking up for my dad being as though I am a daddy's girl. Truth be told he can't do anything wrong in my eyes. Even when it's wrong, he's right! It affected me in a way. Growing up and seeing the violence with him and women molded my brain to believe that a man doesn't love you unless he yells at you and beats on you. That wasn't the only time I witnessed this rage.

I must have been around 10 or 11 when my dad was dealing with a woman named Shannon from Danville VA. I went to stay with them for a week and during that time he taught me how to cook. Shannon had two other children from a previous relationship that lived with her. She thought that she could use me as the live in babysitter while she ran the streets. Well one day her baby fell off the bed and I did not know what to do. He cried until my dad came home. Shannon was not there when he arrived and that was the start of the abuse as far as I had witnessed. He quieted the baby, tended to his wounds, and put him to sleep. In walks Shannon, obviously drunk. My dad looked at me and then at Shannon before he stood up and told her that they needed to talk. She smacked her teeth and sashayed to the back of the trailer. He told me to go out front to play and I did.

Moments later I heard screaming and banging. He yelled at her for leaving me in the house with her child and before I knew it, she yelled out, "fuck your daughter, all you talk about is your damned daughter". Seconds later she came flying through the bedroom window and landed where I was playing hopscotch. Her face was bloodied and bruised. She lay on the ground crying and wrenched in pain. I knelt down to help her wipe the blood from her face and asked what I had done to make her hate me. Before she could respond, I said, "that's what you get"! I ran into the house to check on my dad and asked if we could go home. As soon as we got in the car, the police were making their way down the driveway. My dad told me that he would be going away for a while, and I began to cry.

The police approached the car and snatched my dad out of his seat and slammed him on the hood of his car. I got out of the car and ran over to him crying and Shannon blurted out "That's what you get", before another officer pulled me away from my dad. There were two white police officers that responded to Shannon's 911 call. One had asked whose child I was. My dad said his and Shannon said hers. At that time, I didn't even know my mother's name. The police left me with Shannon and that is where my hell began.

In an effort to hurt me and get back at my father for the pain he had caused her, she would offer me up to the guys she bought coke from whenever she didn't have money to pay for what she wanted. It started with a man touching my underdeveloped chest, then it progressed into him putting his finger inside my private part. No matter how hard I cry for my father or for that man to stop, he wouldn't. Turns out, children excited him. I was fresh, untouched and everything he desired. Shannon sat in the corner, tending to her habits as this man took things to the next level and forced two fingers inside of me while kissing on my neck. I screamed out in pain, and he took that as an invitation to remove his fingers one by one and put his mouth down there. I had experienced my first orgasm by the age of 10.

When it was all done and over with, Shannon told me that I was a woman now. She said next time it will be a little more painful but that's what women go through to please their man. She took me back to her house and demanded that I give her children a bath while she took a nap. About a week later, Shannon was out of money and needed another fix. She styled my hair in spiral curls and dressed me up in a short black dress and high heels. We went back to the same house where the man had made me hurt. She insisted that I would like it this time since I had been opened up before. As soon as we entered the house she smiled and asked where Mike was at.

Someone said that he was in the back waiting for her. She took me by the hand and rushed to the back and burst through the door. Mike was on the bed receiving oral sex from a woman on her knees with no clothes on. He pushed her away when he seen the two of us standing there. Shannon said to Mike, "treat for treat", as she pushed me towards him. He smiled at me from ear to ear as he took me by the hand and prompted me to sit next to him. The girl that he was with asked, "Mike what the fuck is this, that's a baby"! Mike handed Shannon her fix and told her to give him 20 minutes. The girl said, "oh hell no", and proceeded to leave. Mike snatched her by her face and told her to do to me what she had done to him. She kept mentioning the fact that I was a child, but he didn't care.

She lay me down and put her mouth on me while he recorded. I shrieked, moaned, cried and screamed at the way she had made my body feel. It tickled, then it hurt and then it felt good. Before I knew it, some stuff was pouring from my private parts as I shook uncontrollably.

The lady had told Mike that I was ready, and he got on top of me and rubbed my private parts with his penis until it grew hard. He tried to put it in as I screamed and cried out in pain. It would not fit. The woman told Mike that I was not ready and that he was hurting me. He threw her a rock and demanded that she leave us alone. Then he put me on my stomach and told me to relax as he slid his penis inside my opening inch by inch. I could feel myself tear, while he moaned in pleasure. This is what being an adult is all about, is what I kept saying to myself as he defiled me.

Once it was all in, he turned me back over so that he could look at me. He took my legs and placed them on his shoulders as he took away my innocence. The more I cried, the more he moaned and before I knew it, I felt something hot shoot inside of me and pour out. He got off me and yelled for Shannon to come and get me. She took me to the bathroom where I could clean myself up. I sat on the toilet to pee, and it burned. After wiping I noticed that there was blood in the toilet and on the tissue and that scared me. My stomach cramped horribly, and I could barely walk. She said that she was proud of me and took me back home with her.

There was no doubt in my mind that Shannon had done this to me so that she could hurt my father or get back at him. She was filled with so much jealousy, hurt, and anger that she didn't think that what she was doing to a minor was criminal. She also didn't think about the fact that my father would murder her kids in front of her and leave her to carry that pain until he decided to kill her too. An eye for an eye will leave the whole world blind; but my dad never cared much about the world, not even me, only himself.

My hips had begun to spread by the time Shannon sent me back to LuAnn's. I didn't have to say a word because Lu could tell by the way I had filled out that something went wrong. She asked where my dad was at, and I told her that the police had took him because he hurt

Shannon. She nearly had a heart attack as she rushed to contact her lawyer that would eventually help him. LuAnn made a doctor's appointment for me and during that appointment, I told her and the doctor that Shannon let a man touch and kiss on my private area. LuAnn broke down to her knees and cried uncontrollably. The doctor did a rape kit on me as well as testing for STD's. The doctor informed the police and Shannon was arrested within that week. When it was all said and done, I needed eight stitches in my private area and had to be treated for gonorrhea.

Luann was able to get in touch with my father and had set up a visitation with him and the lawyer. She wanted me to tell him what Shannon had done so she took me along for the visit. The only problem was that I had lost my voice! The trauma that I had suffered left me mute for the next year. Lu told my dad what had happened as I sat across from him in tears. He tried to hold me, and I snatched away from him. A part of me was mad at him for leaving me there with her. I felt like he should have taken me back home. More should have been done to protect me. Even as an adult, I am still mad at him and sometimes blame him for everything I've been through. I sat at the table coloring and writing.

When the correctional officer announced that the visitation was over, I handed my father my drawing. It was an image of my father and all his women on one side; and a picture of me on the other side with a bubble coming out of my mouth that said, "I thought you said you can't live without your heart". He would end up serving 13 months before he came back into my life. Once again, he put women before me, and I hardly saw him.

On my 13th birthday, he picked me up from Aunt Lu's house to take me to what was supposed to be a daddy daughter dinner. That wasn't the case because when I got in the car, a woman had introduced herself as Mandy. "Why do you have to include a woman in everything you do with me", I asked. He told me to watch my mouth and to never forget who the adult was and who the child was. I got out of the car! There was no point in me going anywhere with them. I was not interested in getting to know anyone else. It bothered me that he wasn't interested in getting to know me. His daughter! His only child! Before walking into the house, I turned to him and said, "I'm still traumatized by what your last girlfriend did to me, so I'll sit this one out you, two enjoy yourselves".

You would think that he understood my frustrations, but he did not. His only focus was that I had embarrassed him in front of his girlfriend. He yelled at me for me to get back in the car and I yelled back at him saying, "it looks like you're living just fine without your heart so why not just stay the fuck out of my life". With both of us apparently upset, Mandy chimed in and said that maybe it was a good idea for us to postpone dinner. Even though what she was saying made perfect sense; I was still hurt that my father was putting another woman ahead of me, so I yelled out that he was just gonna beat on her too, in an effort to scare her off. Mandy didn't heed my warning at all. About three months had gone by before I agreed to visit my dad and her.

The weekend started off pretty good. My dad was giving me the attention that I needed. This lady seemed to enjoy spending time with me and seeing him bond with me as well. On that Sunday, my dad and I were in the kitchen, and he was teaching me how to fry fish. Mandy came into the house and heard us laughing. She walked past the kitchen and rolled her eyes at me. Shocked by it all, I stopped smiling and raised my eyebrow. My dad noticed and asked me what was wrong. I would not answer him and that made him upset. He poked and poked until I told him the truth.

"Why do you have to keep forcing your women to accept me? Mandy doesn't want me here, she just rolled her eyes at me, and I haven't done anything to her", I said.

"When just now"? Turn the fish and don't let it burn, I'll be back", he said.

The sound of banging and screaming scared me and I ran out of the house. Shortly after that my dad dragged Mandy out of the house by her hair. He picked her up and threw her over the porch banister. Her face was all black and blue and she begged my father to call an ambulance. He drove her to the hospital, and she lied about how she got her injuries. The doctors placed a cast around her upper body because her ribs were broken. Her wrist had been fractured in two places, so she had a cast on her left arm.

After leaving the hospital, he made her go inside the grocery store to get food to cook for that night; because the fish that we had been cooking was ruined. He also made her apologize to me for rolling her eyes. That type of abuse is embedded in my head until this day. Just as happy as I am to see my dad, I am also sick to my stomach. This is the same type of abuse that I endured in my relationship with Montez. Devo never hit me. In fact, he was the kindest, gentlest and most patient soul that I had ever met. My dad was a monster and truth be told; he probably still is.

Nearly three hours had gone by as I sat in the car replaying times I had spent with my father as a child. My most memorable time was the summer when he let me help fix his car. It was his most prized possession. We took it for a test drive after installing the radio. He blasted *Summertime* by *Will Smith* and *DJ Jazzy Jeff.* We rode with the top down, singing along to the lyrics as best we could. I was under the impression that he would be keeping me for the summer. Instead, he drove me to his mother's house. Why? Yep, you guessed it! He was with another woman, and he knew how I would react. I had expected him to meet me at the elephant zoo like we originally agreed upon. However, given the circumstances, I cannot fault him for that. The place was amazing and best of all, IT'S MINE!! Bought and paid for by my dad.

# Chapter 6

## <u>Revelations</u>

We all met back up at the warehouse to discuss what should be done with Aldez and Boone. Certainly, death is easier, however, nearly everyone tied to my case were turning up dead. It would only be a matter of time before the feds started looking in my direction. Last night was the most unbearable night that I've had in my adult life. My brain kept replaying parts of my life that I had blocked out and it scared Dream. She's seen a side of me that no one has ever seen before and did her best to take care of me. I am certain that she feels like she bit off more than she can chew. On this day I reminded her of the warning that I gave her way back when. She was determined to stay in my corner when she could have just gone about her business.

Shit is about to get ugly! Secrets will be revealed, bodies will drop and it's gonna all boil down to the last man standing. Only the strong will survive this storm. My only concern was if I would have to treat Dream as I did

Roxy. I have no room for weak links or casualties. Everyone pulled into the warehouse as if it were a funeral they were showing up to. I'm dressed in all white, whereas Tez, OG, Ken, Roc and Dream, were dressed in all black. Maybe they know something I don't know. Or maybe I do know! Montez stepped to me and asked if I had spoken to our children. Still annoyed with how things played out with him and I, I reached for my gun and warned him that if he said another word to me his body would be the first to drop. I'll never forgive Tez for the turbulence that he has caused in my life. I hate men and he is no exception. The fact that we have children together is the only reason why he is still standing.

Sounding defeated, Montez held his head down while walking away. It was what he said under his breath that caught my attention. "You got all this hate in your heart towards me and I ain't did nothing but show up for you. I'm not the only motherfucker in this room that's got secrets. Shit, your beloved father got the most tea to spill. How come you're not giving him your ask to kiss"?

He walked over to Rocco and asked how Shannon was doing. Roc said, "Ayo how you know my momma cuz". Dream looked as if she had seen a ghost, she went on to say that her mother's name was Shannon as well. She had no idea who her father was though. O.G looked frustrated by Tez's outburst. The room grew quiet before I asked if anyone had any more secrets that needed revealing. I turned to my father and asked how the name of my attacker came up all these years later. I read the room when Montez said what he said, and from what I can tell, it had also shocked Ken. Ken put away his phone and said, "A fool what my baby mother got to do with any of this"? I was about ready to pass out at the thought of us talking about the same woman.

We all stood in silence before Tez would say; "My fault for the outburst! It's just, you know, OG and I did time together and I remember him mentioning a woman named Shannon that had a son named Rocco and a daughter named Mizani". Rocco yelled out to me, "Man, Cole, I told you that I ain't like this nigga when he got out of the car yesterday. I had a weird feeling about him and whole time this bitch got loose lips".

Not that I was trying to defend Tez, but he isn't entirely to blame. I said, "well he heard the shit from somewhere, now didn't he," as I looked over at my father. Ken had that death stare in his eyes, and he focused on O.G. Shit finna go left as soon as he finished processing what he had just heard or whatever he will hear next. Dream had tightened the grip on my hand which told me that something was wrong. I looked at her in suspense and asked what was up. She asked if she could talk to me in private. Unsure of what it could be I responded, "Come on man not you too". We left the room with Ken and O.G going head-to-head over the past.

Once we were away from all the chaos; Dream said, "Baby, please don't be mad at me, but I was adopted when I was five years old because my mother was sent to prison. My birth mother's name is Shannon, and my original name was Mizani. I had a baby brother named Rockwell, but I don't know what happened to him and I never knew my father". So, wait, you're telling me that you were that little girl that Shannon would leave me in the house with to look after? All this time you've been lying to me about who you really were. As far as I'm concerned, you are a part of something that I wish you weren't. Who in the fuck is Dream then? All this time we spent together, and you never once thought to tell me your true identity?

As hurt and betrayed as I felt by Dream, I could not fault her for choosing to keep her past a secret. She worked so hard to leave the past in the past. I understood that wholeheartedly! It doesn't make it hurt any less though. She told me that she loved me and never set out to hurt or betray me. Dream wanted to work through all the secrets and drama and so did I. I had grown to trust her. She was all I had, and I was all that she had. We both wanted to know how this would turn out. No one knew her real identity, so she could choose to keep it to herself or approach her brother and maybe father. I took her by the waist and pulled her into me as I whispered, "I'm with you" in her ear. Spoken like a true co-dependent huh? Dream hugged me and tried to kiss me on the mouth, but I was not ready for that, so I pulled back and suggested that we go and handle business.

Before I could make another move, my thoughts had gotten the best of me, and I stopped dead in my tracks. I said, "Hold the fuck on bro, Ken is my uncle Dream; if that nigga were your father, that would make you my cousin". "If O.G is my father, that would make you my sister", Dream said. I snatched my hand away from her and vomited right where I stood. Either way it plays out, I had crossed a line and there ain't no coming back from that.

In the other room, Ken and O.G were still arguing, and I just wanted answers. I fired my gun into the air. I had no time to waste and wanted to get to the bottom of this DNA mystery. Nothing else mattered at this point. I decided to break the news to Ken. "Hey unc, when I was a little girl, I remember my dad dating a woman named Shannon. At the time, she had two kids, a boy, and a girl. Shannon ended up sexually exploiting me to get even with my dad and was later arrested. Obviously, Rocco is Rockwell. The little girl's name was Mizani; is that your daughter unc"? Ken said that Mizani had been born before he came into the picture. That brought me a bit of relief to know that I hadn't been fucking my own cousin. I asked how O.G ended up hooking up with a woman that he had been dating and Ken said, "It's because your father is a snake like that. He's got to have everything and everyone for himself".

One thing I knew about my father was that he would take the blame when he was wrong, but when he was right, or had something to prove, it's another story. O.G stood up like a proud peacock and announced that he had been fucking Shannon since before she had children. Said something about the fact that he had introduced Ken to her; and like the snake he was, he began a relationship with her. My heart dropped immediately! I broke out in another cold sweat and O.G asked me what was up with me. I said to everyone, "Nigga, this is Mizani", while pointing at Dream. Everyone's face grew in shock and suspense.

"Dad am I really your only child or is there something that you need to tell me?", I asked. His mouth dropped and based on that reaction; I knew all that I needed to know. Dream was in fact, my half-sister. My stomach grew weaker by the second. O.G tried to offer an explanation that all boiled down to him being young, dumb, and full of cum. He went on about how the two of them hooked up and fell out when she told him that she was pregnant. He gave her money for an abortion because I had just been born and he wanted to work things out with my mother. He talked about how she was a cokehead and that upset Rocco enough for him to swing on OG.

No one bothered to break it up. I assumed that everyone in attendance felt like OG had it coming. The problem is that once OG got to beating Roc's ass, Ken jumped in! Ken ain't never been there for his son until now. It was a bittersweet moment that would end abruptly once Dream fired her gun into the air. She has some choice words for OG. She asked how come he never came back for her even after he realized that Shannon did not have an abortion. She was also able to recall a time when he was there, shortly after Roc had been born. OG always showed up for women. Never his child, well children. To my surprise, she even remembered the day when Roc fell off the bed and I didn't know what to do.

That childhood memory was a huge trigger for her because she knew what her mother had done to me. Not only that, but Shannon had also sexually exploited Dream. There we stood, sisters, with the same exact trauma; from the same woman, born from the same man. I'm not sure how our relationship will play out after today. Surely intimacy and affection were off the table for me. Dream on the other hand, did not seem to care about us being sisters. She still pushed up on me in front of everyone. Maybe she's still too traumatized to fully process what had just taken place. I on the other hand wasn't with none of the fuck shit. That's little sis to me. It's not going down ever again.

O. G's phone had rung, and it was LuAnn with a three-way call with FrootLoop. Everyone was happy that a distraction had come. It was very tense, and no one knew what would take place next. Fruit Loop wanted to know if OG had reached me and if our business had concluded. She also wanted to arrange a visit with me and OG. Fruit Loop was due to be released within the next month. She had already made plans to live with Luann, just so that her parole officer would have a stable address on her. I don't know much about her but I'm willing to bet that she will go back to my dad. They had that Bonnie and Clyde relationship a lifetime ago. O.G still had a soft spot for my mom. I could tell by the way he looked when he answered the phone when she called. That's all he needs is another distraction! Another reason to keep me on the back burner. The funny thing is that he wants to be there for his grandchildren, or so he says. It does not change the way he raised me or interacted with me moving forward.

Now Dream is in the picture and that feels extremely weird to me. The Bear has yet to comment on that matter. It's as if he's deflecting and was ready to get down to the real reason why we were at the warehouse. Dream hadn't said anything about the situation either. She's acting like that wasn't news to her. Maybe she's still in shock, maybe she's hurt, hell I don't know.

Rocco stood up and asked if we all could agree that it was time to do what we came here to do so that we could go on about our business. Ken jumped up and said, "that's the smartest thing that I've heard all day it's about time to distance myself because there's too many snakes in this grass". OG stood up and said, "if you're feeling any kind of way about anything pertaining to me, less air it out right now. What I won't do is stand next to anyone and feel like I need to watch over my shoulder".

Ken said, "Shidddd nigga, that's exactly my point when it comes to you and that weird ass nigga right there" (pointing at Tez). Tez responded nonchalantly, "The fuck nigga, ion give a fuck how any of y'all feel about me. I'm not thinking about none of y'all asses. I ain't show up for no one but Cole. Now if you're feeling any kind of way, you can step to me after we handle this business. Matter of fact, Nicole, lead the way so I can get this shit over with. I want to see who wants work from me. I'm tired of the slick remarks from what's supposed to be, grown ass men. Yeah, I fucked up and you wouldn't be here if it hadn't been for me. I accept that, so let me do what I came to do so we can move past this shit".

Rocco clapped his hands while saying, "Oh this nigga talking mad tough now that he ain't inside. We all know that you are a bitch. You are a bitch now and you were Devo's bitch upstate". I held my head down in embarrassment. Roc ain't have to go that far. There was no need for him to speak on matters that he had absolutely no idea about. He is going by hearsay, and I regret talking to him. Montez didn't say another word. All he saw was red and he attacked. He had gotten in at least five punches before Rocco realized that Montez was whipping his ass. Tez's rage made him overpower Rocco. Those insults made him snap! There was no getting Tez off Rocco. Ken and O.G tried and Tez fought them off and went back to punishing Rocco.

"You don't know what I went through in there man. I fought hard for my manhood for as long as I could. You try being held down by three to four men. Your bitch ass can't even fight. You're the type to hide behind your gun or your daddy. Look! Daddy here and he ain't saving your ass. You talked all that shit and can't even defend yourself. What's to stop me from running up in your ass right now? Your street cred? Can you stop me after being beat to near death? Here, let me show you how it happened. Be glad that it's just me"!

Rocco begged and pleaded with Tez not to do it. I had never seen a man beg and apologize so much in all my life. Roc begged for someone to help him. He cried and sadly, no one came to his rescue. His body hurts so bad from the ass whooping Tez gave him, that he couldn't find the strength to get off the floor. Ken and O.G couldn't do anything to help Rocco because they too understood where Montez was coming from. They knew Rocco had said too much and that he had gotten his powers just by being related to Ken. He needed a reality check that would eventually change his entire life. As bad as they wanted to intervene, they could not!

To give Rocco a fighting chance, Tez demanded that Roc got up to fight him. Tez wouldn't fight back, he just wanted Roc to be able to walk away from it all knowing that he had tried to fight for his manhood. Roc said, "Aight cuz, you got it, you win, I'm sorry, go ahead with that shit bruh, I'm not with the gay shit". Obviously annoyed, Tez said, "Nigga, do you think that I was on some gay shit when I was raped"? He punched Roc three more times, causing him to fall. Then he did the unthinkable! He shoved Roc onto his side and ripped away at his clothing.

Tez didn't care that we were there and pleaded with him not to do it. He forced his dick into Roc's ass. Roc screamed loud enough to wake the dead. Tez shouted, "bitch ass nigga, defend yourself", as he thrusted with force. The entire time he was fucking Roc, he had his eyes on me and me alone.

I could tell that he learned that from Devo because that's the same shit we did. I would be lying if I said that I wasn't turned on. My pussy leaked while he thrusted until he could feel himself cum. Tez pulled out and nutted around Rocco's mouth. He knelt down and said, "bitch ass nigga, go clean yourself up, we got business to tend to", then walked away with only a swag that he possessed.

O.G and Ken had left out of the room long before things escalated. They heard Rocco's scream and knew what Tez had done. Tez knew that there was no getting out of that shit alive. To be honest, I do not even think that he cared to live long. He walked like a proud man but deep down, I am sure that prison has changed him. His experiences are not normal. Filled with sadness, I walked over to Montez and asked if he was OK and if he wanted to talk after we did what we had to do. He brushed me off by saying, "Nah I'm cool, let's just get down to it." "Damn we were always good to talk to each other," I said. He said, "That was before you convinced your baby father to rape me." I insisted that I did not have anything to do with that. "You gotta understand how reckless you had been with me. "No, I am not condoning what Devo did, however, you aren't innocent, and you crossed many people to get to where you are standing right now," I reminded him. His decisions made no logical sense to me. He upset the universe and his karma would not be kind to him.

# Chapter 7

## **All Falls Down**

Everyone had met up in the room that Aldez and Boone were being held in. Once Boone seen my face, she could not help but yell out "murderer". Calling me what I am does not phase me one bit. It frustrated Dream enough for her to walk up on Boone and pistol whip the teeth out of her mouth. This girl must really be an *Edwards*! What in the hell did I just witness? Aldez had turned his head to avoid seeing Boone's teeth fall from her mouth. He caught a glimpse of Montez's face and burst into laughter. Aldez yelled out at Tez for him to unchain him. "I'm telling you right now Montez, release me or everyone here is gonna know our little secret," he yelled!

We all stared at Tez and wondered what kind of leverage Aldez had over him. Montez kept his cool and told me to say the word. I think I speak for everyone when I said, let the man speak! Tez would try to overtalk me, by insisting that we just get everything over with. Dream pulled her gun on Tez and demanded he shut the fuck up so that Aldez could talk.

"He cut a deal with us a long time ago. We pressed him about a situation unrelated to you. He agreed to hand you over to us after the murder of Nakyta. Montez said that he wanted to make you suffer for shooting him and killing Nakyta. Him and Luann took an immunity deal. You are never gonna see your kids again because an emergency custody hearing took place in your absence and custody was awarded to Tez's mother. Luann would still have access to them, but you will not! Not until the oldest child is 18 years old; that is around how many years you are looking at so far; kidnapping federal agents, well you will be looking at life, so you better be holding a full deck", Aldez said proudly.

Before he could say another word, Tez has shot him to death. He turned to look at me and insisted that it was not what I was thinking. There is nothing that he could say to me that would justify him taking my kids away from me. My aunt too!? O.G chimed in, "Baby girl what do you want us to do? We are all in your corner. I know you are hurt but we can't leave no stone unturned here".

*"Well, you were locked up with him and he shared a lot with you; So, tell me, did you know that him and Luann gave me up and cut a deal*? I asked.

"Baby girl, that is why I am here for you and asking what you want me to do! O.G exclaimed.

"The only thing that matters to me are my kids and he took that away from me. He could have just left me alone. It made no sense why we were here. Why does he hate me so much? What is up with my aunt? Why does it seem like everyone is against me? Take a deep breath. Inhale, hold for five seconds, exhale and repeat, I said to myself; anything to keep me from reliving the night that all this shit started. Over a piece of glitter! A piece of fucking glitter," I yelled while staring at Tez and demanded that he explain himself.

To hell with all these pointless ass emotions! "Pops, take the gag off Boone. Let's see if she has something to say". To my surprise, she said that everything Aldez had said was true and that I needed Montez alive if I ever wanted to see my kids again. Ms. Lydia, his mother, moved shortly after she gained custody of my children. Only Tez and Lu know where she lives.

"Man, fuck all of this shit," Rocco yelled while pointing his gun at Tez. "Man, cuz, I am sorry to hear how shift playing out for you; but maybe it's not a bad idea that you are not in the kids' life for a while. This nigga raped me cuz, he gotta go, Roc said before firing two bullets into Tez's chest. Rocco was in fact hurt. Tears flowed down his cheeks as he stood, frozen in his thoughts. I walked over to hug him, and he fell into my arms and broke down.

"It is fucked up cuz, he ain't have to do that shit man. My father ain't do shit to help me. Your father ain't do shit to help me. Imma kill the both of them," Roc said, through all his crying. He stood up and laughed it off. "I don't want you thinking I'm a bitch ass nigga," he said while wiping his eyes. There is bad blood between those three. Roc not gonna let that shit go.

"Untie that bitch and put her in the trunk, we need her alive. She knows where my kids are," I yelled!

Boone yelled out that she would not tell me anything. I locked eyes with Dream and seconds later, she had shot Boone in the head at point blank range. Dream yelled at Ken, O.G, and Rocco to help get the bodies into the same car. We got the bodies together and Ken went to start the tow truck that was in the warehouse. OG hooked the car up to the tow truck and we all agreed to follow Ken out of state so that we could burn the bodies. Rocco decided to ride with Ken. I am sure they had some talking to do. Dream and I decided to ride with O.G, our father.

The drive was long and quiet. I forced myself to sleep the moment O.G turned on the radio and asked Dream to tell him something about herself. I slept for hours and when I woke up, we were deep into South Carolina. Ken's truck was parked in some woods about three quarter miles away from where O.G had parked. Apparently, we would have to walk the rest of the way to get to Ken and Rocco. O. G's reasons for that, was that he didn't wanna get his tires dirty. I decided to walk alone. Dream tried to catch up to me, but I managed to avoid that. She knew why I was distant with her.

Heavily breathing, I asked Rocco if he emptied everyone's pockets. Ken doused the bodies and car and gasoline, and I struck and threw the match. There's gotta be an address in someone's wallet or phone, I thought to myself. I just have to find it. The moment that I began to walk over to the tow truck, Ken and Roc began to argue. Ken said from Roc to let that shit go and with tears in his eyes, Roc said, "a real father will kill to protect their child. You ain't do **** to help me pops"! Roc shot Ken, right where he stood. It was not until Roc stood over Ken to watch him bleed out that I realized how fucked up in the head this whole ordeal left my cousin. His mental state was unpredictable at this point. Roc turned the gun on O.G and that's where shit got ugly. Cause, NOT MY FATHER! FOH!!!!

"What are you doing Roc"? How do you think this gon play out for you baby, c'mon, put the gun down for me," I pleaded!

He asked me why I wanted to save O.G knowing all that he did and did not do as a man and father. More importantly, he was hurt that O.G did not stop Tez from violating him.

"We family cuz, don't make me do this," I yelled as I pointed my gun at Roc.

"*I do not blame you for wanting to kill me little cuz. I do not even want to live any more. I cannot live with myself knowing what that man did to me, but this nigga right here,*" Roc said before shooting at O.G.

My response was to open fire, and I did, hitting Rocco three times and causing his body to collapse onto the floor. Dream took the gun out of my hands and said that I did Roc a favor by taking him out of his misery. O.G squirmed on the ground, grimacing in pain.

"Well, I guess you are gonna have to get your precious car dirty after all. Are you hurt bad? How many times were you hit"? I asked. O.G insisted that he would be okay and asked that I ride him to his car so that he could get some shit from his trunk to patch himself up with. Dream and I helped O.G into the tow truck and took him up to his car. He said that we would have to burn Ken and Rocco's bodies in the tow truck. The only catch was that we would have to do it in a different location. That meant that one of us would have to drive with corpses sitting next to us. Dream volunteered and I got the impression that she was trying to impress our dad. I did not have any objections though! I helped Dream load the bodies in the truck and instructed her to drive to a remote area that the *Edwards* family owned in Raleigh North Carolina.

O.G asked if I had any plans on how I would get my kids back and I told him that I had no idea where to start other than with LuAnn. Everything seems to have to go through her first, like she is queen of some shit. LuAnn would be the first stop after we left Raleigh. In the meantime, I had already tossed the cell phones of my recent victims. While on the road, I found two potential addresses in Boone's wallet and an address with a pin code and Aldez's wallet. Dream is gonna draw attention to herself if she keeps swerving in and out of her lane like she is doing. OG blew his car horn at the tow truck until Dream got sense enough to realize we were signaling her to pull over.

I told dream that she was swerving, and she said that the engine was dying. We are not gonna make it to Raleigh. I asked if she thought she could make it to the local park about four miles away and she said that she would try. It took about 30 minutes to get to the park because the truck's engine kept stalling. Once there, we noticed that children were still out playing. O.G suggested that we wait until nightfall and we both agreed. Three hours would pass before we could burn the truck. After it was all done, we piled into O. G's car and drove towards the nearest hotel.

Once there, Dream would check in so that we could shower and rest up. O.G would shower first because he was bleeding through his clothes. Dream stood up and walked towards the door. I asked where she was going, and she said that she was going to walk over to the adjacent hotel and get it wrong there. That made perfect sense because even though the room had two beds in it, we could not all share the same sleeping space. I did not wanna stay here with O.G, so I asked if I could tag along with her, and she agreed.

I prayed that she would not be on any exclusive shit; however, her heart was not willing to accept the fact that we were sisters and could not be in a relationship. Once in the room, she started nagging me about going back to the way things were before we learned that we shared the same father. A part of me wanted to function as if I did not know the facts because I had developed a strong love for Dream. However, the facts are the facts, and I cannot change that, nor do I want to. Dream went into the bathroom to take her shower. I sat on the bed and rolled about three blunts and poured the both of us some drinks. It had been a long day and we both needed something to help us unwind. I would doze off before Dream got out of the shower. I woke up to find her grinding on my lap. No doubt that she was still able to turn me on, but all that ran through my head was that she was my sister.

She leaned into my face and kissed me. I do not know if it was the weakness in me what the freak in me that made me kiss her back. Before I knew it, we were engaging in sex and there was nothing that I could do about it. I will admit, I was not turned on like that was before learning that she was my sister. She was though, it was as if she did not know what a thing about me. A part of me like that! She straddled my lap and breathed heavily in my ear. Dream asked that I just forget that I had learned of us being sisters. She wanted that connection that we developed months ago. I too wanted that connection because I felt alone and up against the world. I needed someone that was there for me, and I knew that it was her.

My mind wrestled with the fact that I was engaging in sexual activity with my half-sister. When I say half-sisters, it makes it seem not as bad as saying sister. The fact that the matter is that I had fallen in love with my sister, and I was clueless as to what to do about the fact. She was still everything that I had wanted in a woman, and I was that woman and protector of which she had dreamed. We had sex that night. Do I regret it? No! Would I do it again? No! I had only done that to help her lower her guards when it came to me. After she went to sleep, I went to the casino of the hotel. There I will meet the most beautiful woman that I had ever laid eyes on. She stood at five feet ten inches tall, caramel complexion skin, long locks down to her waistline, thick hips, a wide derriere. I am in love! Her name was Lyric. The two of us had hit it off before Dream came downstairs and put on a scene.

Completely caught off guard, I told her that her behavior was uncalled for. "We are sister's baby! What are you expecting from me? She did not care about anything that I was saying. All she was caught up on was the fact that we were lovers before we found out that we were sisters. She wondered what my next move would be with respect to finding my children. She asked how sitting in this bitch's face would help me get closer to doing what it was that I needed to get done. Once again, I could not question her whatsoever, because she was right. I was just looking for temporary satisfaction to help me get over the fact that I was hurt and completely caught off guard by everything that took place today. I was like a dog in heat, I just wanted to fuck and nut, over and over, and over again, until I forgot that I had been intimate with my sister.


Dream was determined to scare everybody off. I mean, anybody that looked at me twice, Dream had something to say about it. She reminded me of my first girlfriend in so many ways. O.G had called me on my burner and asked where I had gone to. I told him that Dream, and I wanted to give him his privacy, so we checked into the hotel across from where he was staying. He told me not to get caught up in Dream's web. He needed me to remain focused on the task at hand. MY CHILDREN! After getting off the phone with my father, I called LuAnn to see if we could come to an agreement. She answered the phone with an attitude. I could hear Messiah in the background and that brought me joy. She let me know that my mother would be coming to stay with her, and I asked her how she felt about that.

She was not too thrilled, but she knew this day would come eventually. All the questions that I had asked her had nothing to do with my kids and I wanted to keep her as clueless as possible. I would be on the road first thing in the morning and if push came to shove, that would be one dead bitch. I fantasized about taking my kids to the elephant farm that I had acquired through my dad. There was nothing or no one that could keep me away from my babies. Let them try!

O.G, Dream and I decided to take two days to rest and come up with a plan to get my children. He was still tight with LuAnn, so he called her to tell her that he was coming to swap cars. Once on the road, Dream had asked if O.G ever wondered if she were his child. I asked if they keep their shit to themselves. If we are gonna be honest, they should have had this talk during the two days that we all were idle. I am trying to focus on getting Jenesis, Messiah and Angel. Dream was desperate for answers, and I understood that so I put my Air Pods in my ears so that they could have their privacy. I could still smell Dream's scent on my upper lip and every so often I would rub my finger across her nose. She laughed every time! O.G wondered what we were up to. If he knew what we had done the night before, he would have had a heart attack. Six hours later, we pulled into LuAnn's driveway.

When we rang the doorbell and walked in, Lu looked as if she had seen a ghost. She yelled for my Jeni to go to bed. She asked O.G why he did not tell her that he was bringing company. You know how people that has done you wrong do when you are in their presence? They have a hard time making eye contact with you. They avoid conversation with you, no matter how many questions you may have asked. That is what Lu was doing to me. She only talked to my dad and Dream. I was a fucking ghost to her. Since that is what it is, she has no reason to take up the same air as I. Once again, I made eye contact with Dream, and she understood the type of time I was on. There was nothing more that I needed to say so I asked O.G to get my kids and meet me in the car.

I almost shed a tear as I walked out of LuAnn's house. I knew I would never see her again and she would never see my kids again. My mother would never get the chance to confront her sister. It felt like I was breaking so many codes but, at this moment, I did not care. The fact that I was a ghost to her hurt me. She knew that all that mattered to me were my kids and it did not stop her from driving a knife into my back. I am tired of taking everyone's feelings into consideration while they shit on mine. It has to stop somewhere. Family is the worst, and I will never make the same mistake again. The longer that I sat in the car, the more I second guessed if I was making the right decision. All I hoped for was that Dream would have sense enough to wait until O.G brought the kids out before she killed Lu. My babies have been through enough, they do not need to bear witness to that type of thing.


The front door opened, and I seen my Jeni mini running towards me. O.G had Messiah in his car seat and Angel on his hip. I jumped out of the car and picked Jeni up. The way that she hugged me made me burst into tears. How could anyone want to keep a child away from their parents? This hug was long overdue, and it did not stop with her. Angel reached out for me while yelling, "mama." Messiah cooed and kicked his feet. My heart is filled with so much joy and I could not believe that all my babies were here, in front of me. Moments later I heard a gun go off. Dream would walk out of the house about forty-five seconds later. This reunion had been cut short because Dream had killed LuAnn. That girl was meant to be a hitman. Today confirmed that. O.G helped me get the kids in the car. Before I could get in with them, the police were already making their way down the driveway.

I insisted that my dad take my kids to the elephant farm. If he never heard anything else from me, I demanded that he keep them there, where they would be safe. That man had been in and out of my life since I was a child. The least he could do was be there for his grandkids in my absence. The looks I gave Dream told her everything she needed to know. I was willing to do life over shawty. I was willing to take all charges as long as it meant that she would be safe. I mean, I know that she is my sister, but before all of that, we found love. At this point, that is all that I have to keep me going. The police were so caught up with my capture that they did not notice Dream and O.G pull off with my children in the backseat. They had been gunning for me for over a year, and they finally got their hands on me.

It did not scare me when I thought about being in jail. I can hold my own. The only thing that I worried about was the charges they had on me and how long I would be sentenced. I am certain that O.G had already contacted the attorney to update him on what had taken place at LuAnn's. One thing that I won't do is sit here and play stupid. I knew that they had me on the murder of Nakyta, Al, Judge Conyers, and her husband. They could only speculate on the disappearance of Jesse, Roxy, Aldez, Boone, Ken, Rocco, and Montez. The district attorney would have a challenging time proving shit without any witnesses. That is what kept my head strong. It would only be a matter of time before I returned home. If my lawyer succeeds in getting a specific judge on my case, I will be out in two months tops!

How do you go from having a respectable nursing career to about six felonies within a year? I will tell you how, trusting the wrong people! It could have been worse. I could have lost my life at any point. Right now, my mind was on getting to Lydia. I feel like when she gave me that money and told me not to return until I had taken care of everything, she had already plotted to take my kids away. That type of thing cannot go unanswered. It wasn't for anyone to decide whether I was fit to raise my children. Those are my kids! While in booking at the local police department, the officers joked and laughed at how I was captured. The joke is on them, I thought to myself because now, they are down by two colleagues, and they would spend a lifetime and resources trying to find their bodies.

After they were done taking my fingerprints, they took me down the hall to have my mugshot taken. With all the confidence of getting out filling my mind, I smiled while my photo was being taken. My mugshot picture would speak a thousand words. Even when I am guilty, I am innocent. They had one last trick up their sleeve that I did not see coming. Officer Warren escorted me to my new cell. You would never believe who I was to share a cell with! That is right, you guessed it! FROOTLOOP!!!!! In other words, my mom! She was not happy to see me in there. I chose to look at the brighter side. At least I would get to spend time with my mother before she got out and let my father fuck with her head again…

*"All is well, and I have no regrets, if I had it to do again, I would not change a thing".*

**Be on the lookout for "Can You Listen"**

**Word has it that The Bear, Nakyta and Dream cross paths again.**

Made in the USA
Middletown, DE
18 November 2022

15422358R00070